Spaceports & Spidersilk

October 2023

Edited by
Marcie Lynn Tentchoff

Spaceports & Spidersilk
October 2023
Edited by Marcie Lynn Tentchoff

All rights reserved. No part of this publication may be reproduced or transmitted in any form or by any means, electronic or mechanical, including photocopying or recording or by any information storage and retrieval systems, without expressed written consent of the author and/or artists.

All characters herein are fictitious, and any resemblance between them and actual people is strictly coincidental.

Story and art copyrights owned by the respective authors and artists
Cover art "The Many Dreams of Esther" by Sandy DeLuca
Cover design by Laura Givens

First Printing, October 2023

Hiraeth Publishing
P.O. Box 1248
Tularosa, NM 88352
www.hiraethsffh.com
e-mail: hiraethsubs@yahoo.com

Visit www.hiraethsffh.com for science fiction, fantasy, horror, scifaiku, and more. While you are there, visit the Shop for books and more! **Support the small, independent press...**

Stories

14	Of Mothers and Monsters by Grace Joy Howarth
28	Goodbye, Nathan, Goodbye by Terena Elizabeth Bell
43	The Hailstone Prince by Pamela Love
50	Taking My Eyes to the Shop by Grant Swenson
58	The Golden Necklace by Brad Jensen
75	Slamming on the Brakes by Michael Barbato-Dunn
80	Midnight at Moonville by Diane Callahan

Poetry

27	On MoonBase Lane by Lauren McBride
39	Trogdabogian Dyson Spheres by Corey Elizabeth Jackson
41	Alien Gardener by Guy Belleranti
42	Oops! by Lisa Timpf
48	Frumious Bandersnatch by Douglas M. Jones
60	The Guardian by Goran Lowie

Illustrations

40	Garden Bird by Vonnie Winslow Crist
42	Castle With Crows by Vonnie Winslow Crist
86	Who's Who

From the Editor

Once upon a time, not long enough ago or far enough away, there was an editor. The editor sat in a bright (if somewhat messy) room, at a desk which held not only her computer, but an odd collection of back issues, books, office supplies, hair elastics, drifting tufts of multicolored cat fur, cheap-looking metal pendants, and one very large (but almost empty) mug of tea.

She was frowning.

"What do I have for October's issue? Is there enough spookiness?"

She checked through her list. "Oooh! There's a Halloween story, a ghost story, a really creepy one about eyes, and even a few monstery poems! There are definitely dark pieces here, and thoughtful ones, with hints of pain and sorrow. Nice for the time of year... but maybe too much? Where's the fun, funny, upbeat stuff?"

The editor scrolled worriedly down her list. "Oh, right! Extra-planetary driving attempts! Magical mysteries and mishaps! ICE-COLD PUNS!!!"

She nodded to herself. "This will do."

The editor reached happily for the last swig of her tea, then wrinkled her nose in disgust.

"This *won't* do, though. Not enough left, and what there is has gone cold."

Peeking around to make sure she wasn't being watched, the editor reached out to tap one of the slightly tarnished, obviously fake pendants. The palm-sized, roughly-cast shape of a contented-looking dragon glowed a warm red, and then faded.

The editor picked up her now-full mug of tea, blew away the steam that drifted from the top, and smiled.

"This is going to be a fun issue!"

Pyra and the Tektites
Aquarium in Space

Pyra, age thirteen, is running away from home in the Asteroid Belt because she's not doing well in school. Her parents want to send her to Mars for school, and she doesn't want to go. She sneaks aboard a cargo shuttle, and falls asleep in the hold. When she awakens, she finds herself in free-fall; the shuttle has been seized by the Tektites, a group of rebel pirates . . .

. . . and the adventures begin!

Order a copy of this thrilling adventure here:

https://www.hiraethsffh.com/product-page/pyra-and-the-tektites-1-by-tyree-campbell

Adopted Child
By Teri Santitoro

Imp, now 13, has awakened from stasis by MA, the ship's computer, to find that everyone else has been killed by a highly infectious disease. She is alone on the ship. But she is about to have visitors.

The *Greentown*, a salvage ship, has spotted a derelict and is about to board her for salvage rights. The crew is blissfully unaware of what happened to the people on the derelict. Soon enough they will find out...but will it be too late? And what of the girl who now controls the derelict?

To everyone involved, everything is new... and potentially lethal.

Ordering Link:

https://www.hiraethsffh.com/product-page/adopted-child-by-t-santitoro

The Adventures of Colo Collins & Tama Toledo in Space and Time
By Tyree Campbell

Out on their first date, high school seniors Colo Collins and Tama Toledo are invited aboard a spaceship and offered the chance to intervene in various events in the Universe. These events can range from stopping an asteroid from striking a planet to helping someone find her house keys. But there's a catch: both Colo and Tama have to agree that an intervention should be performed . . . and sometimes they'll have to perform the intervention themselves!

Ordering Link:

https://www.hiraethsffh.com/product-page/adventures-of-colo-collins-tama-toledo-in-space-and-time-by-tyree-campbell

SALE AT HIRAETH PUBLISHING!!!

THERE'S A SALE GOING ON!!!
IT'S STILL GOING ON!!!

BUY ALL THE BOOKS YOU WANT AND USE THIS 20% DISCOUNT CODE: BOOKS2023

GO TO OUR SHOP AT
<u>WWW.HIRAETHSFFH.COM</u>

NO MASKS, NO WAITING, AND WE NEVER CLOSE!

Mellie

The Adventures of a Teenage Vampire

Meet Mellie, an adolescent vampire, as she travels to Italy and New York to discover roots, make friends, and of course get into trouble. Fun adventures for the whole family.

https://www.hiraethsffh.com/product-page/mellie-the-adventures-of-a-teenage-vampire-by-debby-feo

Of Mothers and Monsters
Grace Joy Howarth

"What are you doing?"

Dax's mother was fastening herself into a beige coat, and furrowing her hands into neon orange fluffy gloves, decorated with simpering rabbits. She did not look suitably horrifying at all.

She turned, and a small frown tucked itself between her eyebrows. "Sorry, darling," she said, sorting through her handbag, more interested in whatever was jangling inside than in him. "Work called last minute. I'll have to leave you in on your own for the evening."

"But-" he started.

"I know, I know. Bad timing, right? I'm not happy about it either." She paused her rummaging, offering her hand, and squeezing him into a hug. Her fuzzy gloves tickled his nose. "I really am sorry. Hey!" she reached for a plastic cauldron on her shelves. Inside, bright candy wrappers glinted like gemstones. "You can give these to trick-or-treaters... Make sure that too many don't go missing in *there...*" she patted his tummy and gave a conspiratorial wink, as though they were two spies on the same mission.

Dax didn't feel like a spy. He felt like half of a bad comedy duo, who had just walked into a plank of wood.

She kissed him on the forehead and rushed out, stomping downstairs in her sensible sneakers. "Be good! Don't let anyone in!"

The door clanged shut. Dax was left alone. White paint smeared on his face, hair stiffly gelled, fake blood dripping from his mouth. He spat out his plastic fangs, dropped his cape on the floor, and folded his arms. If his life were a cartoon, smoke would have been pouring from his ears. It was only his absolute *most* favourite, *most* eagerly anticipated day of the entire year. Why did she have to ditch him on *Halloween*?

Their house was on the outskirts of town, miles from where his friends were meeting to knock on doors, stuff themselves with sweets, and howl at anyone lacking treats. His mother had promised to drive him there, dressed in the bat costume that was still in its packaging in her wardrobe.

Grabbing a handful of chocolates, Dax slumped to the sofa. He put on a TV show about witches, which did not fill his veins with even a drop of dread. *Might as well eat a few more candies,* he reckoned, because no-one was dumb enough to trick-or-treat this far in the depths of nowheresville.

Somehow, not even an hour later, Dax's stomach was swollen like a balloon, and every time he moved, it gurgled in complaint.

He fished his hand into the cauldron, and only grasped air. It was utterly empty.

Just as he groaned, dreading his mum's reaction, the doorbell rang shrilly. Dragging his feet, he crept to the door. There was another ring, followed by a heavy knocking. Thumping. Desperate.

Currently, the best excuse he had was that a bird flew through the window and took the cauldron of sweets to use as a nest. She wouldn't believe it in a million years. He smeared the chocolatey stain from his mouth, and swung open the door, offering a grimacing smile.

Only, it wasn't his mum at all. A girl paced from foot to foot on his welcome mat. Her pale makeup was far more convincing than his. It didn't end in a sharp line at her chin. Her parents must have let her buy red contacts, while Dax's mum had said they were bad for his eyes. Her cloak was a heavy, plush, scarlet velvet. It had definitely not been purchased on Amazon like Dax's flimsy bit of material with a cardboard collar.

"We're out of sweets," Dax said, glum. "Sorry." He hoped the trick would be easy to clean up before his mum got back.

"Can I come in?" she asked, eyes darting behind her. "Someone is chasing me."

"Um..." Dax peered around the empty fields surrounding his house. "Who?"

Her fidgeting grew frantic. She pulled the cloak around her face and stared at him. "Someone who wants me dead."

"My mum said not to-" he said, before the realisation of her words truly crashed into him. "Someone who wants you *dead?!*" he squeaked. "Then come in, quick! What're you waiting for?"

He stepped aside and she rushed through, heaving an enormous sigh. "I am eternally grateful," she said. He laughed. Her voice sounded like elderflower cordial, and so formal, like someone from the period dramas his mum watched. She quirked her head to the side, glancing him up and down. "Why are you dressed in such a way?"

He tugged at his garishly red bowtie. "Same reason as you," he said, wrinkling his nose. "Your costume is much better, though."

Her eyes narrowed and she smoothed the long satin swathes of her skirt. "Yes," she said, a little shortly, "Well. Thank you again."

"Erm..." he had never had a friend over to visit before, so was lost with the normal customs. He thought of what his mum did at her monthly bookclub meetings: flipping on the kettle and brewing the tea. "D'you want a drink of something?"

Her eyes flickered to his neck and she frowned. "No, that's not why I'm here."

"Okay..." he glanced around. "Well. Make yourself comfortable. My mum'll probably be back soon... She'll be able to help you."

The girl smiled. Her teeth glinted as sharp as needles, bone white and ferocious. "*Woah*," Dax breathed. "Those are *wicked...*"

She put a hand over her mouth, and eyed him carefully.

"Where did you *get* those?" he continued. "Mine look stupid. And I felt like I was chewing on a tire."

"My father is a dentist," she said after a long pause.

It didn't make much sense but Dax shrugged. "Bet you won your school costume competition. I didn't even get in the top ten."

"I hope you do not find this too improper..." she interrupted, "Do you mind if I invite some acquaintances?"

"Like... a *party*...?" Dax felt a thrill of excitement, overshadowed by the fact he would be grounded for the rest of his life.

"No, not at all!" she protested. "Just some companions in need of help. They are being chased too..."

He hummed. His mum would probably like him to make some more friends, and he could easily deny eating the mountain of candy if other people were there. "Yeah... should be fine..." he said.

"I appreciate it, Dax. Thank you."

She drifted into his kitchen, leaving him dumbfounded, feet glued in the hall.

How on Earth had she known his name?

It was approaching ten o'clock, and despite what the girl had said, it was looking an awful lot like a party in Dax's lounge. He had no idea where all of these people in their outlandish costumes had arrived from. They were chattering loudly, cackling, hooting with amusement, bellowing to old friends across the room. They had brought with them a whole menagerie of black cats, owls, toads, and salamanders. Dax's mum was allergic to cats, so she was bound to be fuming when she got home.

A boy in a werewolf costume had yelped when Dax had tugged the thick pelt of hair on his arm and asked where his outfit was from. Someone dressed as a Victorian ghost floated by, and Dax stared cluelessly at his feet, unable to figure out what was creating the illusion. A girl dressed as a witch complained about the cold, and snapped a ball of fire into her hands.

That was enough.

Dax flung a cup of water over her hands. She gave a cry as she fizzled out, but Dax was more concerned with the state of his home. "Stop it! Everyone stop it! I'm going to get in so much trouble if you burn my house down!" he yelled. The room fell into an icy silence. "This isn't a magic show. Can't you just sit calmly and stop showing off these lame tricks?" He looked sternly to the girl who had first knocked on the door. "I thought you said this wouldn't be a party?"

Her red eyes filled with regret. "Forgive us, Dax. We can get a bit carried away." She turned back to the crowd. "Come on, everyone. Clean up after your familiars... It's not a petshop in here! And water nymphs..." A group of girls with long wavy hair, sodden to their skin, looked at her. "You're dripping all over Dax's carpet."

He glanced down, and noticed that, indeed, there were unexplainable patches of dark beneath their feet.

"Sorry, Verity," one of them said, her dewy cheeks turning pink. "We'll go and sit in the bath."

"Verity?" Dax said.

The girl's eyes widened. "Did I not introduce myself? How rude!" she smiled, her razor-sharp teeth flashing. "I am Verity Bourjeoulais... We really are endlessly grateful that you took us under your roof like this."

"We'd be in a dreadful state without you," peeped a small voice from somewhere behind the sofa.

"The hunter nearly had me!" the boy dressed as a werewolf said. "I thought I was done for!"

Dax blinked. "Hunter?"

"Come on, Dax," Verity said gently. "Do you truly still believe we're all just in Halloween costumes?"

He stared at her. Her marble-pale skin, her red pupils, the impossible teeth, the lack of breath in her throat. Then beside her, the wolfish boy gave a grin, his fangs too enormous to be human. Dax noticed that when he looked closely, he could see the TV playing right through the ghost guy's torso, and the tiny voice had come from a minuscule creature, bright green with wicked looking claws and snakish eyes.

Dax swallowed a scream in his chest.

Then, as though he had been thumped in the head with a saucepan, he fainted cleanly away.

Heart pounding in his mouth, Dax's vision swam. He blinked his eyes open, unsure if he had been asleep for a second or a day. The crowd of monsters, ghosts and ghouls were leaning over, pulling at his arms and murmuring lowly.

"Are you quite alright?" Verity gasped, looming close with her scarlet stare.

He scrambled back, whimpering quietly. "Please don't eat me," he begged, "It's my favourite day of the year! I can't be eaten on my favourite day!"

Verity laughed, and the lights flickered, only highlighting the viciousness of her teeth.

Dax crumpled into a ball, fearing the worst. "If you have to... make it quick..."

But instead of feeling fangs pierce against his skin, the pressure of a cool palm landed on his shoulder. "Humans may call us monsters... but we aren't as monstrous as the stories say," Verity said softly. "If anything, your kind can be so fearful of us, that they turn into the monsters themselves."

"That's why we're hiding," the werewolf said, his yellow eyes surprisingly warm. "There's a monster hunter on duty, and their motto is kill first, ask questions later."

"A monster hunter vacuumed my sister away," the ghost said, wiping at his eyes, "I haven't seen her since 1897."

"A monster hunter nearly took my head off with a sword!" a pallid creature wrapped in bandages said, "It's a good thing it's removable anyway," he reached up and cradled his dismembered head in his arms.

"We all have nasty tales about the hunters," Verity explained, "And the evilest of the bunch, the Head Huntsman, is scouring this very village tonight." She shivered. "Luckily we have a Diviner in our midst, Seraphina..." she gestured to a girl with paper-white hair, and blank eyeballs. "Her Vision told her that the Huntsman has already checked this house, and has moved on to search for prey in the town centre."

Dax turned pale. "The Huntsman was here?"

"Probably just snooping around in the garden," Verity said. "But, all this to say, we mean you no harm. In fact, we owe you a great debt for protecting us in our hour of need."

"Oh," Dax said weakly, head still spinning. "Well don't worry about it," he sat up slowly. "Only my mum'll be back soon, and I don't think she's going to believe all of this."

Verity smiled, and now that Dax was over the initial shock of the fangs, it was a rather lovely smile. "Grown ups can be very stupid about that sort of thing," she nodded, "We'll just say we came over to trick-or-treat."

"Do you have any apples?" the werewolf asked, "We might as well take part in some human traditions since we're here... I've never gone bobbing for apples before."

Midnight approached, and Dax laughed as the werewolf emerged from an enormous bowl of water, a Golden Delicious in his fangs, shaking off drips like a dog.

All of a sudden, Seraphina sat bolt upright, her skin beginning to glow a blinding moonlight white. Her mouth lolled open, but where her tongue and throat should have been, there was only a pitch black hole. An eerie humming scraped gutturally in her chest, and her blank eyes rolled back in her skull.

Verity darted over, inhumanly fast.

"What is it Seraphina?" she said, shaking the girl's limp arms, "What do you see?"

Seraphina began to tremble, twisting, writhing in her seat. "The Huntsman," she said in a voice deeper than any Dax had heard before. "The Huntsman is coming." As soon as the words had escaped her mouth, she slumped, knocked unconscious with the strain of the vision.

The monsters descended into chaos, filling the house with ghostly weeping and shrill shrieks.

"Everyone!" Verity said, but nobody heard. The headless mummy lost his head. The ghost was whirling around so frantically, that he passed right through Dax's chest, making him feel as though he had been thrown into a vat of ice. The werewolf was running, crashing into the back door, trying to burst it off its hinges. A loud clap of thunder. Verity stood on the table, her arms lifted to the sky. "*Don't panic!*"

Everybody stopped in their tracks, looking up to Verity. Their moaning and groaning fell silent.

"Dax," she said clearly, "Please lock the doors and windows."

He darted to the front door and put it on the latch. He shimmied the bolt shut, a squeak of rust piercing his ears. He hoped it would hold against a hunter and whichever evil weapons they may possess.

He ran back into the kitchen where the monsters were. "Now, keep quiet," Verity was saying. "Avoid the windows. If we lie low, hopefully the Huntsman will get bored and leave. It is against The Hunter's Code to scare other humans. As far as the Head Huntsman knows... Dax is just a clueless boy. No hunter would break in and reveal the truth about monsters to a human child."

"I'm not a *child*," he protested, "I'll be twelve next month."

Verity shushed him and flicked the lights off with a click of her fingers. The monsters dropped to the floor and hid themselves under the furniture.

The moon pierced through the curtains, making the whole room look like a ghost house. A chill crept up through the floorboards and spider-crawled across Dax's spine. His throat was tight with tension, chest aching with the heavy-metal drumbeat of his heart.

Sure, he enjoyed trick-or-treating, cheap costumes, and chocolate, but he was starting to think he didn't like Halloween so much after all.

Outside, the gate creaking sounded like a dying groan. A soft crunching of footsteps on gravel. The glow of moonlight was cut open by a shadow. It loomed up close, floating over the wall. Dax and the monsters watched silently, the whites of their eyes flashing in the dark. It was a figure, and unmistakably, in its hands, was the silhouette of a cruel, glinting sword.

Dax gulped. His tongue felt oversized in his dry mouth. He could hear the tap-tap of toes making their way to the front door.

The heavy brass handle cried out as it turned, twisting loosely in place. A fumble of metal. The sharp grating sound of keys in a lock. The door thumped against the bolt.

Suddenly, Dax wished he had barricaded them in. Their lives rested on one measly bolt. If the iron gave way or snapped, it would be game over.

"Hello?" came a voice. "Are you in there?"

The monsters shrunk in their skin, quivering like autumn leaves.

"Dax?" the voice called.

An enormous wave of relief washed over him, like a cool shower after a heatwave. He sat up, his heartbeat returning to normal.

He opened his mouth, but before he could summon breath to his lungs, there was a cold hand covering his lips.

"Don't," Verity said, her voice a fraction of a whisper. "Please."

He wriggled from her grasp. "Don't worry," he murmured back, "That's just my mum home from work."

With wide, wild eyes, Verity shook her head. "It's her."

"What?" Dax squinted.

The door rattled again. Everyone jolted in fright, trying to press themselves deeper into the ground. The shadow returned against the wall, pacing angrily. The sword brandished through the air and crashed into the window, spitting glass shards through the room. One arched and skidded past Dax's cheek, burning in a sharp burst of pain. The monsters smelled blood, their stomachs growling.

It was no use hiding. If they wanted to make it out alive, they would have to fight.

They rose in unison, as quietly as they could. The werewolf's hands split open into foot-length claws. Seraphina's skin fizzled with electricity. The water nymphs readied the tsunami strength waves they could summon. The mummy lifted his arms and started to lumber forwards with his brute strength.

"It's her," Verity repeated, her fangs drawing out, her nails growing into shards of metal. The shadow sawed through the glass with the sword, clearly out for blood. The edge of an orange glove peeped into view. Fluffy. Covered in rabbits. Grasped around the hilt of the sword. "Your mum. *She's* the Huntsman."

On MoonBase Lane
Lauren McBride

Come by my dome -
I'll make some room
in my small home
where friendships bloom.

New friends from Earth
to study stars -
you'll have to meet
my friends from Mars.

Goodbye, Nathan, Goodbye
Terena Elizabeth Bell

Everyone else got to go on migration, everybody. Why last time even John Balley got to go and John Balley's father had said they'd never do it. They'd been final holdouts — live with Earth, die with Earth, that's what his father had said — but still he got to go. The kids were all going now, there were only four left in Nathan's class, and when John Balley left they shut down school for the whole day just to say goodbye.

It wasn't really goodbye, Nathan told Momma when she asked if he was sad. They still have to drive to Florida.

But that night he messaged his Aunt Melinda and told her to look out for his friend — his name is John Balley and he's eight years old but he isn't tall like me — and Aunt Melinda said she would.

Nathan's aunt had been part of the first migration. She'd moved before Nathan was born, but that didn't mean he didn't know her. I'm here for you, Nathan, I love you, she said on a heliocall, and just because I live on a different planet doesn't mean you can't come to me, then asked how Nanny was feeling.

She's okay I guess, and Aunt Melinda said, put your mother on please, but whenever Aunt Melinda called, Momma always told Nathan to say she wasn't home.

Aunt Melinda was a reporter, which meant she got paid to tell people things, Nanny explaining that's why they'd sent her, that while the colony needed scientists and farmers and people who worked with their hands, NASA also wanted somebody there who could share their stories. This made Aunt Melinda a celebrity of sorts, something Nathan thought was cool, but just made Momma mad. They get her opinion on everything, she said, who cares what she thinks about the flares? It's not like she's a solar expert.

But still, the Earth received a heliocast from Aunt Melinda once a week and they'd even hung up a poster with her picture on it at the planetarium down at LBL.

Why LBL was still called that, Nathan would never know. It used to stand for Land Between the Lakes, Nanny had said, stretching out her side, explaining how when she was a girl there'd been water, two whole lakes filled with so much water they had to dam it up — the government building the planetarium on a stretch of land between them — and when Nathan said, well there aren't any lakes down there now, Nanny sighed, there used to be. Lake Kentucky was biggest in the state. We'd go swimming there, she told him, and when Nathan asked, what's swimming, Nanny brought up something else.

When I was a little girl, she said, the planetarium held light shows, and Nathan asked what kind.

Oh you know, turning up her heating pad, they'd play Pink Floyd or Beatles music and point colored lasers all around, and when Nathan said that sounds dumb, Nanny said I guess it was. But people weren't so interested in actual astronomy those days.

He did not ask why they were interested now. He didn't have to. They'd learned all about it in school. Miss Bell had handed out an infosheet printed on real paper. NASA wants y'all to bring this home to your families, she said, standing tall at the head of the class, and Nathan wondered if Aunt Melinda had wrote it.

"The effects of radioactivity from solar flares are far more complicated than scientists initially understood," Nathan tripping over words like "initially" and "effects." He knew what they meant but they were hard to sound out and when he asked his teacher for help, she said it's okay Nathan, you've got this. You know those words.

The infosheet also said only one migration was left, something Nathan did not know, and this made him even madder. His Aunt Melinda was an original colonist, first to board the USS Hope, the very first shuttle to go, Momma saying I'm sure the captain and crew were already on there, but when they showed the recording of people getting on it in class, she was the first person Nathan saw. Nathan had family in the colony, he should get to go. NASA didn't like splitting families — that's what Miss Bell had said — but John Balley got to go and his family didn't know anybody there at all.

Nathan's teacher was a never-leave, but not for the same reason John Balley's dad used to be. If I go, she told Momma once, who would teach these children? But now almost all of Nathan's class was gone and she didn't seem that pleased with her decision.

The day the migration took off — the one John Balley was on — they sat in class and watched it, live from Kennedy Center, and when the rocket lifted, heading up straight in the air, Miss Bell began to cry.

It's okay, he wanted to say, the man on tv said successful launch, but then he heard his teacher whisper, goodbye.

So that day Nathan went home and told Momma, if there's only one migration left I think Miss Bell should be on it, and then Momma looked at Nanny and Nanny said, Miss Bell huh?

Sometimes older people, said Momma, well it's hard for them to migrate, and Nathan thought Miss Bell isn't old.

Still, his teacher would have to apply. Everybody did but them. John Balley's father had gone down to the courthouse and signed on a line, filled out pages of applications and forms — but Nathan and Momma and

Nanny, why they didn't do a thing. A man in a uniform just brought their tickets to the house every year, coming up the drive in a long black car, and when she saw him, Nanny would look at Nathan and wink. See the USA in your Chevrolet, she'd say before she opened the door.

After the man left, Nanny would set the tickets on the table and at night, after she thought Nathan had gone to bed, she'd touch the edges. There was always a rim of dust around the sides, it formed as each migration passed, Nanny lifting all three the day after take off, leaving a square clean spot on the table where they'd been.

That night — the night after they watched John Balley leave at school — Nathan dreamt of tiny dust particles rising out of empty lakes, of clouds kicking up behind the army man's car, coming in the windows, the windows of the house, and when he awoke the next morning he still felt it.

Are things, he messaged Aunt Melinda, on the colony clean?

It took five years to get there — that's what Miss Bell had said — and you could either sleep or stay awake the whole time, and when she'd said that, John Balley had opened his eyes real wide, and Nathan said not the whole time-whole time, goober. She just means not everybody gets frozen in that tube, Miss Bell asking Nathan to please be quiet, saying it's okay John, you'll be fine, even giving John Balley a hug. The people who stay awake still get to sleep at night, it's just some people want to go to bed and not wake up until they get there, letting John Balley know his father would decide, either way you'll be okay. Still though, he looked a little scared, and it made Nathan feel bad that he thought this, but he thought it anyway: he thought if that were me, if I was the one who got to go, I wouldn't be afraid.

It's a hard trip Nathan, Momma told him, standing at the kitchen counter, mixing bread powders in a bowl.

Other kids go just fine.

It's not you I'm worried about, she said, but when Nathan said, then who, Momma looked out the window and ignored him.

Momma was worried about everything. She was worried about the truck, the house, making-do, Nanny's back. She even obsessed about his lessons, constantly asking Miss Bell, how'd he do today, as if any day at school were really that different from the next. All they talked about now was migration, migration and survival skills for any kid who stayed, Miss Bell telling Nathan, I know you want to go. The whole world, sweetheart, knows you want to go. But not everyone will get to and just in case you don't, I need to make sure that you all have the information you need to live the best possible lives here, then she turned to the next student.

That night Nathan sent a message to Aunt Melinda saying if he didn't get to migrate, could Miss Bell at least have his ticket, then Aunt Melinda heliocalled: Your mother, Nathan, she said. Get her on the line. Now. And don't tell me she isn't home.

It was the first time he'd ever seen Aunt Melinda mad, her face scrunched up just like Momma's, and when Nathan left the room, he could still hear her in the hall. His teacher, she yelled, I got those for you. Then Momma said something muffled and Aunt Melinda calmed down a bit, I can try. But if I do this, she said, he's coming with her. Unless you want him to die? How many times do I have to tell you? She'll make the trip fine.

Die? Nathan didn't want to die. Why would he die? That didn't make any sense. But before he could ask, before he could barge in the room and say, why would I die, Nanny saw him in the hall. Nobody ever learned anything from eavesdropping, she told him, that they really wanted to know. Now put your oxygen mask on and we'll go to the planetarium for a show.

But the whole drive down he was silent, putting pieces together he did not understand, different parts of multiple puzzles combining and shifting at once. Nanny, he asked, why doesn't Momma want to migrate, and, actually I think she does, Nanny said, then Nathan was silent again. When they got there, the planetarium was almost empty. There used to be summertime star parties and lectures about the flares — like when Nathan was really little — but today there was just one man, only one other person in the whole place, and looking up at the ceiling, at the telescope in its dome, Nathan felt sick to his stomach. Nanny, he said, can we go home?

That night he dreamt of the dust again, clouds as big as their house, whooshing from the igniting shuttle, launching into space, of Momma and Nanny left standing on the ground. But when he went to school the next day, he forgot it.

Nathan, I can't thank you enough, Miss Bell said. Of all the things, brushing her hand across the top of his head.

What, Nathan told her, did I do, and all Miss Bell said was you were you.

Who else would I be?

Exactly, and then Miss Bell smiled. Now class, if you could all turn your handbooks to chapter seven, "storing water and food in a fallout shelter," then when Nathan got home, Momma asked, did Miss Bell seem particularly happy today, and Nathan said, yes, why actually she did.

They must have gotten her a ticket, that had to be it, the final launch window had just been moved up. Do you want him to die — whatever that'd meant — Aunt Melinda had come through.

In the weeks that followed, Miss Bell had a pep in her step and concentrated on her other students more. There were two girls and one other boy left in Nathan's class and one of the girls was going, her father had gone down to the courthouse to sign, and when she said, I hope you're coming with me Nathan, he told her, I do too.

But as the launch got closer Nathan noticed neither Momma nor Nanny looked like they were ready. I don't believe this, he said. It's the very last one Momma, my very last chance, Nanny in the dining room again with the tickets, not touching the edges but staring — sitting in her chair, bent at the waist, pushing her butt out all the way so that her eyes were on level with the table, folded completely into herself. Nanny, don't that hurt your back?

But Nanny, she didn't say a word. She didn't even move. She just sat there, looking at those tickets.

Momma, his mother said, that's not doing either one of us any good.

That night, Nathan did not dream of anything. Instead, he lay in his bed and watched out the window, looking at the darkness and what lay beyond. It was rolling. The earth, the space, the dust, the world — everything in the universe was moving oh so slowly while Nathan, he lay right here. He could hear them, Momma and Nanny; they were in the kitchen fighting, Nanny telling Momma, you have to, Momma saying, how could we, Nanny saying something back that Nathan could not understand, words he did not know, words that belonged on an infosheet, but no matter what they meant, he knew he had to go. Family does not leave family, Momma said, but Aunt Melinda had gone. Aunt Melinda had got to migrate and there wasn't any reason anybody needed to be left behind, why at this point even Miss Bell had her ticket.

None of this makes any sense, he told Momma the next morning, I heard you and Nanny. Then Momma got this look on her face and reached out to hug Nathan tight. I'm sorry baby, she said. I'm sorry was all she said.

Nathan had not seen Momma pack. She must have done it while he was at school, as he sat in Miss Bell's class and learned about vegetable canning and "emergency care of the sick and injured: chapter nine," coming home every day to give Momma and Nanny evil looks, but still someone had packed. A suitcase had been ready all this time — and another one, too — and when they headed out the door for what Nathan thought was supposed to be the goodbye ceremony at school, well, Momma took those two suitcases out of the house and put them both in the truck.

What's that, Nathan said, are we going, but he wouldn't let himself get excited. There was something building inside him that would not, could not be excited: There weren't enough bags and where on earth was Nanny?

Isn't Nanny coming, he asked, and Momma said no.

Momma! Nathan ran in the house, Nanny where are you, screaming from room to room, then there she was at the computer, looking at pictures of children, kids laughing and playing in water. This, she told him, pulling Nathan in her lap, is swimming. Then Nanny cried.

She cried and cried until Nathan thought she would never stop, more water he was sure than Lake Kentucky had ever held, tears drenching his face, wetting his hair, Nanny, he said, it's okay, but he knew it wasn't. Nathan might be a kid but he wasn't dumb: You're not coming.

No, she said. I'm not.

Then Nathan, he put his hands around her neck and refused to let go. Even when Momma said, it's time, he refused to let her go. He held and he cried and Momma had to pull and at one point Nanny said, it's okay, baby you're hurting my neck, but still he would not let go, Nanny reaching around, loosening his hands, releasing his fingers one by one, but still — Nathan did not want to go.

Trogdabogian Dyson Spheres
Corey Elizabeth Jackson

Trogdabogians, bipedal amphibians,
Lifespan a million years,
In aim to travel galaxies
Have built gigantic spheres.

Each sphere is larger than a sun,
Each holds a sun within.
As one the sun and Dyson ship
Through space together spin,

Locked in a magnetogravitic field
Together, and never undone.
Bypassing wormholes, the ships
    enfold space,
Bilocating spaceship and sun.

Trogdabogian Dyson spheres are
Vessels for suns, and their plan
Is to forge to the end of the universe
Where they countless far galaxies span.

Garden Bird
Vonnie Winslow Crist

Alien Gardener
Guy Belleranti

Humans plant flowers in gardens.
My alien friend plants himself instead.
He says he must get extra sleep
And that Earth's dirt makes the
    very best bed.

So he digs until he's buried.
After a week I'm worried he's dead.
Suddenly he bursts into sight
Looking healthy green from tail to head.

Castle with Crows
Vonnie Windslow Crist

Oops
Lisa Timpf

Screams ring through the castle,
inspiring dread.
Annoyed, Princess Andrea
smacks her head—
she must have forgotten
to warn her guests
about friendly blue monsters
under their beds.

The Hailstone Prince
Pamela Love

Long ago and far away, a castle stood at the foot of a snow-capped mountain. One summer's day, young Prince Sven of this castle's royal family told his parents that he was bored. "Furthermore, I cannot bear the heat." He dramatically wiped the sweat from his brow. "This very day, I shall climb the mountain to its peak, where the snow never melts."

They yawned and waved him off as they fanned themselves. "Just be back in time for dinner, my boy," the king told him.

"Yes, you won't want to miss dessert," the queen agreed.

So the prince headed up the mountain. First he rode his horse, a noble chestnut named Thunderhoof. About halfway up the path ended, and Sven dismounted. From here on, the prince decided, his own two feet must carry him. Giving his horse a pat on the withers, he said, "Back down to the stables with you." Knowing a carrot would be waiting for him, Thunderhoof departed.

As the prince continued, the way grew icy and ever steeper with every step. Finally, Sven had to climb on all fours or turn back. Having come so far, he refused to give up.

At last he reached the summit. He shouted with triumph, but then began to pant with weariness and shiver with cold. He clapped his hands to warm them and looked around for shelter. When he spotted a small cabin, the prince struggled through the knee-deep snow until he reached its door, knocking once, twice, and a third time.

The door was flung open by a tall, whitehaired lady in a rather rumpled dark dress with a ruffly white apron. "Who disturbs my rest?"

"For—forgive me, madam. I—I must beg you to let me warm myself by your f—fire for an hour so I can make it back down the mountain. One hour's rest only; you have the word of a p—prince." Sven bowed deeply, and clenched his teeth to keep them from further chattering. Etiquette had always been his best subject.

She sniffed. "Bah! What use have I for a prince's word? Indeed, what use have I for a fire?" She shoved open wide her door on its creaking hinges. To his great disappointment, Sven saw nothing inside the cabin but a rocking chair, certainly no fireplace. "I am Mother Winter, who sends snow and sleet during their season. Have I not earned my summertime slumber?"

Sven opened his mouth, then closed it. His etiquette tutor had never covered this particular point.

Folding her arms, Mother Winter went on, "Nevertheless, I shall come to your aid. If you like, I can send you back home far more swiftly than you could travel yourself."

Delighted, Prince Sven nodded, for his legs and arms were aching. Then he felt his pains turn into numbness and his entire self shrinking. Mother Winter chuckled. "Off with you, Prince Hailstone!" And she picked him up and flung him over the mountainside.

Down, down, far and still farther the pumpkin-sized chunk of ice fell, past clouds, rocky ledges, birds in flight, and the tallest of treetops, until the hailstone prince landed with a thud in the soft soil of his own castle's kitchen garden, not an arm's length away from the cook.

Now, she was there trying to decide what dessert to prepare for the queen, who had requested a cool treat due to the heat. Although startled by the hailstone, the cook was pleased at its convenient appearance. "Just the thing! I shall make ice cream for Their Majesties. What could be better?"

Turning to the kitchen boy, the cook said, "Fetch your mallet and smash this hailstone into bits no bigger than the tip of your littlest finger. Set them in a bucket for me."

Woe is me! thought the hailstone prince. He tried to explain but his mouth was gone. He tried to flee, but his legs were gone. (He didn't know why he couldn't hear, since his ears were gone too, but that was the least of his worries as the boy picked him up.)

In the kitchen, the boy set the hailstone prince carelessly right at the table's edge. Just as he raised the mallet over his head, Sven tumbled off. The kitchen floor wasn't quite level, and so the hailstone began to roll across it and soon went out the door.

"Come back!" shouted the kitchen boy, and ran after the hailstone. But now that the icy prince had begun to roll, he found that he could keep on going, so he did just that.

He rolled past the cook. She made a grab for him, but Prince Sven slipped from her fingers and rolled on all the faster.

"Stop that hailstone!" shouted the cook to the knight guarding the open drawbridge. He tried to stab it with his pike, but it skidded away from him and rolled right into the castle moat, splash!

"Fetch it out, Sir Knight!" said the cook. "I need it to make ice cream for the royal family's dessert."

"Nay, for my armor would rust," said the knight. "Fetch it out yourself, Cook."

She shook her head. "Nay, for I never learned to swim. Fetch it out, Kitchen Boy."

"Nay, for I was hired as kitchen help, not as a moat man," he said pertly. He looked around for someone *he* could order about, only to see a creature covered with dripping weeds drag itself out of the moat and onto the drawbridge, with a dreadful groan. The kitchen boy shrieked with terror and hid behind the cook.

"I have solved your problem by fetching myself out," said the prince, for he was himself again. The friction of rolling and the warmth of the water had melted him, restoring Sven to his original form.

The knight, cook, and kitchen boy all gasped when they recognized his voice. (It took some time for them to recognize his face, since Sven was well entangled in the weeds and had some difficulty removing them all.)

Somewhat confused, the knight, remembering his own lessons in etiquette, raised his pike in salute. "Hail, Prince Sven!"

The prince winced. "Hail? No, never again."

Frumious Bandersnatch
Douglas M. Jones

"Beware the Jubjub bird, and shun
The frumious Bandersnatch!"
-- Lewis Carrol, "The Jabberwocky"

Unfurling flaggins breezed all blue;
Champagne salawfing lips and tongues;
The Jabberwock's unhead was hung;
They praisoned beamish boy days long.

Gnarled woman creaked her finger forth:
"Not klain all, that boy; two monsters wait
instood the jungle narth." But boy
blinked left and right and skittered way.

Instead, an ink-haired girl then raised
boy's sword and flooned it down at once.
"No need for steel. My squad will squelch
it with a trick so nonce."

Bwen twilight came, three girls set out
and scaled the nacklish cliffs; their torches
yulled the Bander's eyes; its legs
blurred wide and dripped a pinkish plorch.

It found the girls all digging deep a pit.
It sploked upon them, yawking like a cat.
Their digging was a ploy. They feigned
a screech, led monstank through the plats.

But when it almost grooned their hair,
they roped upto the palms. As Bandersnatch
glared up, a cliff unkloked beneath its toes;
It flooooooooped then burst upon the jagged
gulch.

With colored banners high and wide,
again champagne splooched every turl;
the village cheened and glorfed all night.
New starkists here, our gladsome, glossomed
girls.

Taking My Eyes to the Shop
Grant Swenson

Everything breaks and can be repaired or replaced. I learn this lesson daily when I fix cars with my dad.

Our garage holds two cars and one truck in various stages of completion. The most desperate one is little more than a shell, waiting for a complete overhaul. The diagnostic equipment telling us what needs to be fixed sits in one corner along with stacks of boxes holding new parts. Plastic drapes section off the back area for painting. I love to mess around with the painting equipment. Tool racks line the other corner. I'm responsible for keeping this area organized. I gather what is needed for the next repair and put away the tools at the end of the day.

"Hey dad, I finished repairing the headlights," I say, wiping grime from my fingers on a dirty rag. "Can I paint the fenders next?"

Dad rolls from under a beige 1983 Toyota Pickup. His gray coveralls are well worn. "Your last two paint jobs were splotchy. Don't you practice all the time? Is everything okay with you?"

"I'm fine. Honest. I'll keep trying until my painting is perfect." I don't tell him I find it difficult to focus while painting. The parts are blurry, and I don't see where I miss spots.

"We can work on it together after I fix the suspension. Hand me a 12 mm wrench."

The wrenches are neatly sorted on the work bench, but they are fuzzy. I can't read a single letter or number. I pick randomly and hand Dad a wrench.

Dad laughs. "Very funny." He hands back the wrench. "Give me the correct one."

"Right. It was just a silly prank." I scan the work bench, but nothing makes sense.

The side door opens, and Mom storms in. "We need to talk."

Dad sits up. "What did I do this time?"

"It wasn't you," Mom says, glaring at me. "I just got off the phone with Ronnie's teachers."

My stomach clenches. I don't get in trouble often, but when I do, it's end of the world level bad. "Which ones?"

"All of them," Mom says, gathering her hair in a bun. "Your grades are slipping. They said you might be having trouble reading, but I know you're a good reader."

"It's nothing," I say. "I'm fine. I promise to work harder."

Dad grabs five wrenches from the work bench. "Let me try something." He holds them up. "Pick out the 7/16-inch wrench."

I squint, but the numbers are blurry. I can't tell one size from the next. Guessing, I pick the wrench in the middle.

"Wrong," Dad says. "I think your eyes might be broken."

"My eyes aren't broken," I say.

"Well, they certainly need to be fixed," Dad says.

"I'll make an appointment with the optometrist right away," Mom says.

The next day, Dad and I enter the optometrist office. Everything is clean and bright, but out of focus. I'm scared. Are my eyes broken? I feel like a car waiting for the mechanic to rip out my headlights and replace them with new parts. I don't want new eyes. I like the ones I have.

I hide by the wall of glasses while Dad checks me in. I notice movement out of the corner of my eyes. When I turn around, I don't see anything odd. Am I imagining things?

The hairs on the back of my neck stand up. Someone is watching me. I just know it. I spin around and catch a pair of hazel eyes blink out of existence. Picking the frames off the hook, I examine the wall, but it looks and feels normal.

I set down the frames and back toward the entrance. I'm not sticking around in this bizarre place.

Dad spots me and says, "Hey, don't go running off yet."

"I'm fine," I say. "My eyes are fine. I don't need to see the optometrist."

Dad guides me to the front desk. "At least let them run a diagnostic on your eyes."

A diagnostic test is what I'm afraid of. When we run one on the cars, they always reveal what parts need replacing. Glancing back, I see a fuzzy pair of mechanical eyes behind an oversized pair of glasses wink at me. What kind of doctor's office is this?

The technician wearing a short white coat calls my name and leads me to the back room.

"My eyes are fine, really," I say to the technician. "This will be a waste of time."

"If that's true, this will be a breeze," the technician says. "Don't fight the process, and you'll leave here better than you entered."

What do they mean by process?

The technician directs me to a small, dark room with big machines. I stare into one box and click a button when a tiny light appears. This is hard. I know I missed a bunch.

When I gaze into another machine and hold my eyes open, a bright flash snaps a picture of the inside of my eyes. After my eyes adjust, I see a mechanical creature with headlights on its head giggling. I shake my head, and the image disappears. Was it real? Who's watching me?

In another room, the optometrist flips between glass pieces and asks me to read the letters. The fuzzier the image, the more I think I see something peeking from behind the last row. After what seems like forever, I finally read the bottom line of letters. For a moment the world is clear again.

The optometrist says, "Interesting. I need help on this. Please excuse me for a minute." The optometrist leaves the room.

My heart races. What's wrong? Why are my eyes interesting?

The wall behind me opens like a garage door, and two mechanical creatures with fenders for legs and headlights for eyes drag me from the room.

Is this real? Is this part of the process?

They strap me into a reclining chair on a conveyor belt, and I click forward. The wall closes, trapping me in a humongous room with a green neon sign flashing "Body Shop."

In one corner, a kid checks out a rack of legs. A creature connects wires to a body in the middle of the room and checks the signals on a monitor. In another corner, a kid examines an array of arms. What kind of place is this?

I struggle against the tight straps. "Let me out of here."

A digital voice says, "His eyes are broken. They need replaced."

I roll past a table displaying eyes in every color imaginable. The eyeballs glance at me in unison and roll around seemingly excited about becoming my new eyes.

"My eyes are fine," I yell. "Don't take them."

A small mechanical creature with splotchy fenders and giant headlights circles my chair. It leans me back and picks up a tool with spinning blades and a suction cup. "This won't hurt at all. What color eyes do you want?"

I slip an arm from the straps and unbuckle. Sliding from the chair, I scream, "I want my own eyes,"

Everything and everyone in the body shop freezes and glares at me. The kid checking out replacement legs yells back, "Stop making a fuss. They gave me new eyes last year. I have the coolest eyes now. They're different colors." He blinks, and for a moment his eyes glow yellow.

This isn't normal.

"Get back here so we can fix your eyes properly." The small mechanical creature snaps at my shirt, but I escape its grasp.

I race away from the eyeball table and knock into the monitors in the center of the room. The door to the optometrist office is closed. How will I get out?

Mechanical creatures from every section of the body shop close in on me. I grab a couple of hip joints to keep them at bay, but they don't act like they're worried I'll do any damage. I pull a couple of tools from a wall organized with dozens of strange looking mechanisms, but I don't know how to work any of them.

I back into the corner. The mechanical creatures reach for me. I shove them away, but I can't keep this up much longer.

Where can I go? Something must open the door. I spot a glowing red button along the far wall. I hope it works.

I plow over a creature. Its arm snakes out and snags my ankle. I hit the ground and shake free from its grasp. I pull myself to my feet moments before my pursuers pile on me. I race past the kid checking on arms. I duck under a creature swinging a new arm at my head.

Charging straight for the button, I dive and press it. The door to the optometrist office opens slowly. Light pours into the dark space.

Racing across the body shop, I fake out the small mechanical creature with the big headlights. The replacement eyeballs track my movement. They look sad I'm leaving.

The garage door grinds to a halt. Behind me, a mechanical creature grins and releases the button. The door closes again. I stumble across the conveyor belt. A creature dives at my legs, and I leap over it. I roll under the door right before it slams shut.

I hold tight to the chair base and catch my breath. Sweat drips from my forehead. My body aches. I need to get out of here.

I hurry from the room and smack into the optometrist.

"Woah there," the optometrist says, holding a pair of glasses. "Is everything okay?"

"Don't take my eyes," I say, covering them. "They aren't broken."

The optometrist laughs. "Of course, they aren't. They just need a little help."

"I do need help," I say, peeking through my fingers. "I can't see anything clearly."

The optometrist hands me the glasses. "Try these on."

I slip on the glasses. The world isn't fuzzy anymore. Everything is crystal clear.

I run into the waiting room. "Dad, my eyes are fixed. I can see clearly again."

Dad sweeps me into his arms. "I knew you'd be good as new. Plus, those frames make you look cool."

"Do they really?" I say, checking my image in a mirror.

"These glasses are temporary," the optometrist says. "You can pick out any frame in our stock, and we'll make sure they help your eyes exactly how they need to be helped."

"Thank you," I say.

I examine the wall of glasses and don't see any eyes glancing back at me. Did I imagine the body shop or is it still back there waiting for the next kid who needs a new pair of eyes? I might never know.

I pick out a cool looking frame, and the technician adjusts it to fit my face. I cannot wait until the new glasses arrive.

Until then, I return home to schoolbooks I can read again. The letters and numbers make complete sense. My schoolwork improves to the delight of Mom and my teachers.

More importantly, I don't make mistakes when I help Dad in the garage, especially when I paint the (END)

The Golden Necklace
Brad Jensen

    Clare was starting school in a small rural community in the Alpine region of Germany. All the children in this village had lived there all their lives, as had their parents, their grandparents, and their great-grandparents. They did not see many new people move in. On her first day in her new school, her teacher introduced Clare to her classmates and then asked her to take a seat. The school was old and had old wooden and brass desks that were set to the floor. Each one had a number in brass on the side of the desk. At the back of the class were a few extra tables that had been set up. These were larger and two children had to share one table. Clare saw that desk #13 in the middle of the room was empty. She walked to the desk and sat down. Everyone in the classroom gasped.

    The girl at the desk next to her said under her breath, "You can't sit there!"

    Clare was so surprised that she jumped back up. As she looked around all the kids were looking at her. She was very confused. What had she done wrong?

    "Maybe it would be better if you sat in the back, Clare," the teacher said.

There was only one place left, but she had to share it with a very large boy who already took up most of the table. She had to squeeze into what room was left. She did not like this at all!

"Hi, my name is Flip," said the very fat boy. Clare did not reply.

However, at lunchtime, she sat with Flip and found that he was a very nice boy.

"Flip is a strange name," said Clare.

"Well, it is actually Philip, but Flip is my DJ name," said Flip.

Clare wondered why Flip needed a DJ name, but she decided not to ask.

"Why couldn't I sit at that desk?" Clare asked Flip.

"I am not sure," said Flip, "but everyone knows it brings bad luck."

"I don't believe in bad luck," said Clare. After class, the teacher spoke to Clare. "How is everything going, Clare? Are you fitting in well?"

"Yes," said Clare, "but I want to know why I can't sit at desk number thirteen." "Oh, it brings bad luck. Even when I was a child and went to school here, no one sat there. My parents said that they thought that it had to do with a girl who died there a long time ago."

"A ghost?" said Clare, "I don't believe in ghosts."

"You are a brave girl," said the teacher, "but you should be careful. There is a reason no one has sat there."

The next day, Clare told Flip at lunch what she had learned.

"Oh, I am sure it is haunted!" said Flip. "There is no way that I would ever sit there. I don't even like looking at it."

"I want to know more about this girl that died." said Clare. "Where can I find out more?"

"At the library," said Flip. "We can go on the way home after school."

When they got to the library, Clare and Flip discovered that they had pictures of all the old newspapers that had been printed in the town. With the help of the librarian, they found an article that said *School girl dies under mysterious circumstances.* There was even a picture of their classroom. At desk number thirteen sat a pretty girl with long hair wearing an old-fashioned dress. The article said that her name was Jennifer Lightly. However, they could find no further information about the girl or her death.

Clare looked sad.

"I know," said Flip, "I can ask my parents! They know everyone in town. Maybe they know more information."

The next day, Clare walked into class. She strode over to desk number thirteen and sat down. She looked around the class as if daring anyone to say anything. All the students looked shocked or afraid. Even the teacher looked afraid. No one said anything for a long time even though the bell had already rung. The teacher then started the class.

After that, all the students in the school avoided Clare. They acted as if they were afraid of her.

"It's just the bad luck," said Flip, the only classmate who would even look at her. "They are all afraid."

After lunch, the clock on the wall fell to the ground and broke into many pieces. Then later the fire alarm went off because there was a fire in the school cafeteria. The teacher sent the children home early. As they were leaving, a classmate tripped and fell down the stairs. Clare rushed to help her. "Get away from me!" The girl screamed. "This is all happening because of you!"

On their way home, Flip and Clare walked together through the dark woods. "Oh, I almost forgot to tell you," Flip said, "my father told me that he had heard of the mysterious death of Jennifer Lightly but no one liked to talk about the details. He said that Jennifer's father was still alive, although he is very old, and he lives in the villa on the edge of town."

Clare thought and then said, "Then we will go and visit him."

"Ok," stammered Flip, trying to be brave. Over the next few days, strange things continued to occur at school. Then one rainy night, Clare was sleeping in her room when suddenly her dog ran into her room and started barking wildly. Clare jumped up and saw that her window was wide open and the rain was coming in. Clare was sure that she had closed it when she went to bed. She also noticed that the spot on the rug by her bed was wet. Clare shivered as she pictured someone standing there, watching her as she slept. She petted her dog and carefully closed the window. She then went back to bed, but could not sleep.

The next day, Clare told Flip what had happened. Clare and Flip decided that they would go and speak to Jennifer's father that weekend. Then they would have time to visit the villa at the edge of the town. That day, Flip had a music class and could not walk together with Clare, so she had to walk through the dark woods back to her house by herself. As she was walking home, she heard distant footsteps following her. Clare turned around and saw that someone was following her. It looked like someone wearing a long white coat with their hood up over their head. Clare felt a tingle going up her back. However, the ghostly figure was far away, and besides, Clare did not believe in ghosts. After a few minutes, Clare heard the footsteps again. She turned and saw that the figure in white was much closer to her. How did she get there so fast? Now, Clare was afraid. She did not want to meet this figure in the woods by herself. She started walking faster. Soon, the steps were right behind her! She turned quickly. The hood fell down from the white figure and she could see that it was a girl about her own age. It was Jennifer Lightly! Clare felt Jennifer grab her arms and then she heard her yell "WHY ARE YOU SITTING AT MY DESK!" and then the ghost disappeared. Clare ran the rest of the way home.

The next day, Clare told Flip her story. Flip looked ill.

"Maybe you should stop sitting at that desk?" Flip suggested weakly.

"No, " said Clare "I want to get to the bottom of this. I want to walk home alone through the woods again today. Can you let me go alone and then come along later?" "OK," said Flip although he looked very afraid.

Clare walked alone again through the dark woods. Again, Clare saw Jennifer's ghost following her. Again, she saw that Jennifer was much closer, and again, she heard the footsteps directly behind her. This time, Clare spun around and grabbed Jennifer's ghostly arms.

"I know you are called Jennifer, Jennifer Lightly."

The ghost looked surprised. "What happened to you, Jennifer?" Clare asked.

"I... I don't know," said the ghost. She thought for a while.

"Something happened to me in class. I was a girl, just like you. And then I was a ghost... I don't remember. I didn't know where to go. The only place I like to be is at my desk. That is why I don't like other people sitting there...."

"I will help you, Jennifer. We will go and talk to your father. Maybe he can tell me more."

"My father? I should very much like to see him. When you see him could you please tell him that I miss him very much?"

"Of course," said Clare.

"I have to go now," said Jennifer and then disappeared into the fog.

Clare was walking back home when she heard footsteps behind her again. She turned quickly and scared Flip.

"Flip, what are you doing? You scared me to half to death!"

"You told me to come later," protested Flip.

"I did, didn't I?" Clare apologized. She told Flip what had happened and they made plans to go and visit the villa the next day. Clare had told her parents that she was going to visit Flip. Flip told his parents that he was going to visit Clare. Instead, they both when to visit the villa at the edge of the village. The villa had a large metal gate and high walls. Flip and Clare could see a beautiful, but overgrown garden in front of the largest and most beautiful house that Clare had ever seen. Clare rang the doorbell. An older, distinguished-looking gentleman came to the gate.

"Yes, what do you want?" the man asked harshly.

"I am sorry to bother you, Mr. Lightly, but I had some questions..." Clare began.

"He is PROFESSOR Lightly, young lady, and of course, that is not me. I am much too young to be Professor Lightly. I am his servant, George."

George did not seem young to Clare, but she did not say that.

"Could we please speak to Professor Lightly?" Clare asked. "We have some questions we would like to ask."

"Professor Lightly is very old, you know. He never has any guests...."

"Please, George, it is about his daughter. I am sure that he would like to talk to us. We promise not to be too long."

"Well, his daughter is a sore topic with the good Professor. However, I don't see what harm it could do. It might be good for the Professor to talk to someone other than me." George led them through the garden. There were many beautiful plants and trees and statues. One statue, in particular, attracted Clare's attention.

"That's Jennifer!" Clare blurted out.

"Why, yes," said George, "how did you know?"

Clare did not answer but admired the statue as she walked past. It looked just like the ghost that she had met. Professor Lightly was laying in bed. Clare had never seen anyone that was so old.

"What can I help you children with?" Professor Lightly said with a raspy voice.

"We want to ask you about your daughter, Professor. What happened to her?"

"What? My daughter? Why... why do you want to know what happened to her? That was so long ago...."

"It is not so much me who wants to know. SHE wants to know." Clare said, "She sends her love, by the way, and says she misses you very much."

Clare then told the Professor the story of how she met his daughter. The Professor listened with tears in his eyes. "My Jennifer? It was my fault. I never she have brought it home. She found it and brought it to school. Then she was gone. Gone forever and it was my fault."

"What is it?" asked Clare "What did she find?"

"The golden necklace. You see, I am a Professor. I teach archaeology. I spent a lot of time in Egypt. One time, I found an old grave. In it, there was what I thought was a strange mummy. But instead of a mummy, it was a stone statue wearing an intricate necklace."

"And you brought the necklace back with you?"

"Yes, it was very odd. It had the face of a woman who had snakes for her hair. The eyes were made of rubies. I have seen necklaces like that, but never in Egypt. Sometimes the eyes would glow."

"And Jennifer brought it to school?"

"Yes, I had hidden it, but she must have found it. At school, they had asked each pupil to bring something from their parents' work to show to the other kids and say what their parents did for a living. Clare must have found the necklace. She took it out in class and then put it on...." The Professor began to cry.

"Yes, go on, what happened?" Clare pressed on.

"You saw when you came in. You saw what happened to my sweet Jennifer. She is standing out there in the garden. I called the Director at the school and sent some men to pick her up. She loved the garden, so I put her there."

"She turned to stone?" Clare said.

"Yes, and it was all my fault. If it wasn't for that cursed necklace...."

Clare thought for a while and then thanked the Professor for talking to them. She and Flip turned to leave.

Clare had a sudden thought. "Where is the necklace now?"

"I don't know," said the Professor, "maybe it turned to stone too?"

On their way out, Clare looked closely at the statue of Jennifer Lightly. There was no necklace.

Clare and Flip were sitting together at lunch. "We have to find that necklace," Clare said.

"Why? I don't want to touch it. I don't want to turn to stone," said Flip.

"I don't know why. I just have a feeling. If we destroy the necklace, maybe we can reverse it," said Clare. "We have to try."

"But where can we find it?" asked Flip.

"The Professor said that he called the School Director and then sent some men to pick it up. We can ask the School Director what he knows." said Clare

"OUR School Director? Well, he is old enough. Maybe he is the same one?" said Flip.

"Let's ask him," said Clare.

In the Director's office Flip and Clare sat and waited for the Director to come back from an important meeting.

He stormed into the office moving quickly for such an old man.

"Well, children, what is it? I don't have much time," the Director said.

"We wanted to ask you about Jennifer Lightly." Clare said. "Were you here when the uh, accident happened."

The Director stopped and looked over the brim of his glasses. "Yes, it was most tragic. Most unusual. We don't like to talk about that here. Now if you could excuse me...." The Director gestured toward the door.

"The golden necklace, what happened to it?" Clare blurted out.

"Ah, yes, there was something about a golden necklace I believe. I heard it was very unusual. A woman's head with snakes for hair- very fascinating inscription on the back. Uh, I have no idea what happened to it. I never even saw it myself. Now, I have some very important work to do, so I have to ask you to get back to your classroom...."

Flip and Clare were sitting together again at lunch. Luckily none of the other kids wanted to be anywhere near Clare so they could talk without anyone else listening in.

"I guess we are stuck," said Clare. "No one knows where the necklace is."

"The Director is lying," said Flip. "I bet he stole it."

"What? How do you know?" said Clare. "You heard how he talked about it. He also mentioned the inscriptions on the back. How could he have seen them if Jennifer had still been wearing it?"

"That's right! Flip, you are a genius," said Clare.

"I also noticed that he had a safe in the wall behind the picture. It stuck out too much. I bet that is where he keeps it."

"Yes, we will break in tonight and open the safe. Wait! How do we open the safe?" said Clare.

"Leave that up to me," said Flip.

That night, after saying good night to her mother, Clare snuck out of her window and met Flip in the dark woods. They both quietly made their way to the school. When they got to the director's office, all of the doors and windows were locked.

"Let me try," said Flip and pulled out some tools. After working on the door he said, "I got the lock open, but the door is barred on the inside. We will never get in here."

"Wait, I have an idea. I will be right back. I am going to go and get some help," Clare said with a smile.

Clare made her way to her classroom and quietly opened the door. There, as she expected, was Jennifer, sitting at desk number thirteen and looking glum.

"Hi Jennifer," Clare said. "we spoke to your father. He sends you his love."

"You talked to Dad?"

Clare quickly explained what had happened and what they had learned. "But now we need your help, Jennifer. We need to find the necklace and destroy it. Can you help us?"

Flip was still trying to open the door when Jennifer and Clare returned. He looked at Jennifer wide-eyed as she went through the wall of the Director's Office. Soon the door opened. Flip rushed to the painting and confirmed his suspicion that there was a safe behind it. He pulled out a stethoscope and placed it on the safe.

"Where did you get that?" Clare asked Flip.

"I got it from my Mom. She uses it for work."

"Your Mom is a safe cracker?"

" No, a Doctor. Now be quiet so that I can get this open."

It took Flip a while, but eventually the safe popped open.

"You are a genius, Flip," Clare said with a smile.

"There it is," said Jennifer. "I recognize it."

Flip carefully pulled the necklace from the safe. He held it as if it were a poisonous snake. He seemed relieved to hand it off to Clare. Flip carefully closed the safe and put everything back in place.

Clare looked at the woman's head on the necklace. She gasped as the ruby-red eyes started to glow and quickly stuffed the necklace in her pocket.

"Aren't we going to destroy it?" Flip asked.

"Not here, not now. Tomorrow, at the villa. We need you there, too," she said, addressing Jennifer.

"But we have school tomorrow," Flip protested.

"We are going to skip school," Clare said with a smile.

Clare and Flip snuck back through the woods and back to their homes. Before Clare went to bed, she pulled the necklace out of her pocket. The ruby red eyes glowed and she had a very strange and very strong feeling. The necklace was telling her to put it on. She felt her hands moving to her neck as her dog came barking into the room. Clare quickly stuffed the necklace under her pillow and then sat on it the whole night.

* * *

Clare, Flip, Professor Lightly, George, and Jennifer were standing in the garden of the villa around Jennifer's petrified body. "Clare, I think you should have the honors," Professor Lightly suggested.

She took the necklace and placed it on a rock. "Let's hope this works," she said, and then struck the necklace with another rock. The eyes flared red but nothing else happened. Clare felt the urge again to put on the necklace.

"Quickly, Professor, do you have a hammer?" Clare said, trying not to stare at the glowing eyes.

"Yes, George, in my den. You know the one?" said Professor Lightly.

"Yes, sir. Right away sir." George said and then strode purposefully away.

In a few moments, he returned with the most unusual hammer that Clare had ever seen. It was encrusted with jewels and gold and had inscriptions all over it. Clare raised the hammer over her head, hesitated a moment, and then brought it crashing down on the necklace, splintering it into a thousand pieces.

Everyone looked at Jennifer. At first, nothing seemed to be happening, but then Jennifer's ghostly body began to disintegrate like a fog being blown away by the wind. The fog was being blown toward the statue, however, and the crowd looked in amazement as the stone slowly changed color until a flesh and blood girl was standing on the pedestal. Jennifer jumped down and hugged her father. Everyone was in tears.

* * *

Clare and Flip shared a table at the back of the class. Clare didn't mind anymore that she didn't have much space. The bell rang and the teacher rapped on her desk for attention.

"Children, we have a new student joining us today. Please give a warm welcome to Jennifer!"

Jennifer smiled and waved to Flip and Clare and then made her way to sit down at desk number thirteen.

Slamming on the Brakes
Michael Barbato-Dunn

When the aliens abducted him, Josh Brenningham had been just a few days shy of his 16th birthday. More importantly, he was just a few days shy of getting his learner's permit.

Of course, he missed his parents and (to a degree) his snippy younger sister, Marna. He yearned even more for his closest friends, Todd and Justin, and the nasty but hilarious text messages they'd exchange. He longed to play his main and five or six alts on World of Warcraft. And to see the fleeting, curious glances from Celeste in his physics class.

But nothing pained him quite so much as not having the chance to learn to drive. He'd imagined it since he was five, bashing into friends in go-carts at the St. Lucius summer carnival. At first, race car drivers fascinated him. Eventually, though, Josh's daydreams were more of the ordinary sort: upright at the wheel of his father's SUV, steering in and out of slower cars, running through yellows and the occasional red. He saw himself heading to the mall and to Scoop's for ice cream. Better yet, to school in the morning -- friends stepping off buses would watch in envy as he pulled into the lot. He pictured himself taking Celeste to an after-party in Farmington Woods, accelerating over Halston Road late at night, gliding through its sharp curves and steep inclines, then slamming on the brakes when they arrived.

Now, three years after Josh was snatched away (perhaps it was thirty; the space-time continuum perplexed him), his disappointment was tempered by the irony that he was traveling infinitely faster, and far greater distances, by piloting the sturdy shuttle he'd stolen from his captors.

To call this "driving" was perhaps a stretch. There was no steering wheel, and the controls in the cockpit made little sense. Yet the auto-navigator readily comprehended his language and responded precisely to his commands, and Josh thrilled in ordering the craft to swoosh and swoop and glide from system to system. The array of screens that surrounded him mimicked a front windshield, and the stars passed by in thin white bursts. When Josh entered a star system, the shuttle slowed to sub-light, but even then the planets passed in an eye-blink. Fast. Very fast.

Yes, this was so much more than mere driving: he was at once a starfarer, an explorer, a commander. The first human to traverse the galaxy.

And all without a learner's permit.

* * *

The aliens were broad-shouldered with grey, wrinkled skin and tufts of white hair on pointed chins. Their pink eyes were masked by looping lids. Narrow hips and tiny sticks of legs framed the inverted triangles of their bodies. At night they sang screeching ballads and drank thick vials of an orange-red liquid that made them intoxicated. They smelled wretched.

Clearly, they were not scientists. Josh had faced no examinations, no poking or prodding, nor had he been confined to a room or cell. He reasoned they were traders or pirates, and that their sole reason for abducting him was profit. He called them Click-Clacks, a name that captured the odd sounds of their staccato speech.

Whatever their intent, the aliens treated Josh as a curious animal, as humans might treat a newly discovered breed of dog. They allowed him the run of the dim, dank ship, and they would cackle uproariously as he darted throughout the corridors and cabins. He was, it seemed, simply an object of intense amusement.

Josh worked hard to perpetuate the clownish impression, all the while studying the ship and its workings. Early on he had found the shuttle bay unlocked, and none of the Click-Clacks seemed aware of how much time he spent in that chamber. Or that he was devising a plan.

Then one night, as his captors slept off their drunkenness, Josh escaped into the silence of deep space.

* * *

He slumped back in one of the awkward cockpit seats and closed his eyes. His departure had been weeks ago (or years — he couldn't be sure; space-time, and all that) and he fought exhaustion. Steady beeping from the center array of controls signalled his arrival in yet another star system.

He had travelled through hundreds since fleeing his captors, usually three in a single day-night cycle. He kept track by scratching marks in the cockpit wall with a wrench-like device he'd found in the cabin. The lines covered an entire bulkhead panel.

The auto-navigator began what was now its regular routine: a swing by the first planet, close enough to the star to scoop an abundance of plasma fuel, then outward at a steady clip past the second planet and toward the true goal – the third.

"Faster," he commanded. He needed to rest and to eat another bowl of the Click-Clack's sickly paste-gruel, so he had little desire to inspect this system at a measured pace. And he had little desire to bear another round of disappointment.

In moments Planet B appeared, a brown-red dot on the center screen that quickly shot off the far edge of the right monitor. Josh cursed his own impatience. He should slow down the craft. He should take his time. He should--

Planet C was suddenly upon him. Josh leaned forward and squinted. A smudge of blue-green with swirling patches of white, blurry as the stars themselves. Then it was past him, off the edge of the left monitor, gone from view.

It didn't matter. He didn't need to order a replay of the fly-by. He knew.

Home.

And in that instant — not with his foot on a pedal, but with a determined command shouted to an alien circuit board — Josh Brenningham slammed on the brakes.

Midnight at Moonville
Diane Callahan

My brother Derek has a tongue like a knife. That's what Dad says, anyway, and right now they're throwing around words sharp enough to leave scars.

"No son of mine is gonna live that kind of life." Dad's slurred shouts bleed through the pantry door, where I'm hiding. I was getting my almost-midnight snack, but I jumped in here as soon as their footsteps pounded into the kitchen.

"I never asked to be your kid," Derek yells. "Just like I never asked to be—"

"Get outta my house." Dad's talking so low I have to hold my breath to hear him. "You don't belong here."

His words stab my gut, even though they aren't meant for me.

Slam. Derek's out the front door. I sigh so deeply my elbows swing out and topple a tower of canned green beans. A heartbeat later, Dad's flinging open the pantry and staring at me, tomato-faced.

"Is he gonna come back?" I manage to whisper. I've never been as good at talking back like Derek. I can't even yell at the toaster when it breaks.

Dad shrugs, but his eyes look heavy. "Hope so."

He goes into his room, and the lock clicks shut. For the rest of the night, he'll be stewing in his "anger juices," as Derek says.

Truth is, I think my brother's leaving for good this time. He left his phone on the table, like he doesn't wanna be found. The little clay owl I made three years ago in third grade that sits on the kitchen windowsill must've flown off with him, because it isn't there anymore. That stings, since I made it to keep away bad thoughts.

The cold night air bites through my clothes as I slip out the front door. Taillights shine in the driveway. A car door shuts, and I shrink behind a bush. Derek storms past me without a glance.

Derek's yellow hatchback—Miss Daisy, he calls her—belches exhaust in the driveway. I slink toward her, dive into the back, then lie across the floor, hidden in the dark. When Derek returns, he throws a flashlight in the backseat. Miss Daisy lurches, and her bald tires fling gravel.

He turns on the radio, and "hippie music" bounces through the speakers. Usually, he sings along at the top of his lungs, but he's quiet now. It bothers me, that quiet.

He's always talking about music like it's his ticket straight out of Vinton County, to sunshine and greener pastures. I've never really thought about leaving. Where would I go?

But Derek seems to know where *he's* going. Miss Daisy climbs a hill. I don't even want to blink in case I fall asleep.

The car stops. I pop my head up—the clock says it's five minutes till midnight.

Out the windshield gapes the dark mouth of a big stone tunnel overgrown with creeping vines. "MOONVILLE" is carved at the top, barely visible in the headlights. The railroad has been abandoned for years, but everyone in these parts of Ohio knows this place—it's where people die and leave their ghosts behind.

Derek gets out and walks toward the tunnel, carrying the flashlight. He disappears inside.

I wrench open the car door. "Derek!" I hiss. His light disappears. He must be on the other side now.

I close my eyes and run—into the tunnel. Into the darkness.

"Derek! Come back! Don't—" I nearly jump out of my skin when I open my eyes and see a train heading straight at me. I trip on a railroad tie—part of tracks that weren't there before.

My blood feels like it's hardened to stone as the train screams down the track.

Strong arms yank me out of danger. The train screeches to a halt. Struggling to catch my breath, I look up at Derek.

"How did you—?" Derek starts, his eyes wide. "Never mind. You shouldn't be here."

"Where's 'here'?" I ask.

Derek rubs his neck. "The midnight train from Moonville."

"But—"

"Get on if you're going!" a man shouts from the train doorway. His hat and uniform, like the rest of him, look grayed out, like he's a drawing instead of a person. And the train isn't a storybook train—it's white as bone and scarred with rust, the warped metal looking like it's fallen to pieces and been put back together too many times.

"You should leave," Derek tells me.

I shake my head. "I'm coming with you."

Derek huffs but lets me follow him up the metal stairs and inside. There's only one other passenger in the rows of shiny black seats—a woman in an old-fashioned dress staring out the window, so faded she's almost a shadow. The air is so thick with the smell of flowers that it makes me think of a funeral.

"Where are we going?" I ask Derek.

"*We're* not going anywhere. I just need to leave. You should stay. You're only twelve."

I cross my arms. "And *you're* only sixteen. How's that different?"

"Because I'm not wanted. And there's only one place for unwanted people to go."

I frown. "You're not unwanted."

Derek puts his hand on my shoulder. "Liam, get off the train. Go home. I left the keys in Miss Daisy."

"So you're really never coming back? But you don't even have your stuff with you!"

"I won't need it, where I'm going," he says softly.

"I don't understand."

Overhead, the conductor's voice echoes from nowhere and everywhere. "Next stop—the afterlife!"

The door hisses shut.

I whip around to face Derek. "The *afterlife*?"

He sighs. "You heard Dad. I don't belong here." His eyes are shiny, and the only time I've ever seen my brother cry was when I broke my elbow so bad it dangled off me. His tears make me angry—not at him, but at the world, at my dad's constant sneering, at all the excuses people make to be uncaring.

"That's stupid," I say, louder than I've said anything before. "What's Dad's problem with you, anyway?"

"He doesn't like that I . . . I . . ." Derek hangs his head.

"That you like girls *and* guys?"

My brother looks at me like I just threw up on him.

"I notice stuff," I say. To me, Derek has always been this way. I saw him hold hands with one of his football buddies, and it didn't make me disappointed or sad. It just *was*.

The train isn't moving yet, but I doubt we have much more time.

All the mixed-up thoughts inside my head spill out. "You know what I like best about you? You never let anyone else tell you who to be. You're just you."

Derek stays quiet for a moment. "I don't know if home is home to me anymore," he mumbles.

"But you can always get off the train."

We sit, just breathing.

"Plus," I say, "I want my owl back."

Derek looks a little embarrassed as he takes the owl from his pocket. "Just wanted something to remember you by, I guess." He hands it to me, but I shake my head.

"You need to put it back yourself."

He throws back his head and laughs—really laughs. Before long, I join in, because he's so obnoxiously loud that I can't help it.

The train rolls forward.

"You staying? Or going?" I ask hurriedly, almost afraid to hear his answer.

Derek pulls a cable beside the window, and the wheels screech to a halt. "I'm staying me, but going with you."

As the train door yawns open for us, he puts the owl back in his pocket.

Really, I don't mind if he keeps it forever.

Who?

Sandy DeLuca has written novels, several poetry and fiction collections and a few novellas. These include critically acclaimed works such as DESCENT and MESSAGES FROM THE DEAD.

Her visual art has also been published in books and magazines. It has been exhibited throughout New England and in New York's Hudson Valley.

She lives in Rhode Island with several feline companions, including a black cat named Gypsy and her two sons, Gemini and Leo.

She is currently working on a new novel, poetry and a series of large-scale expressionistic paintings. She spends some of her free time volunteering at a local food pantry, photographing abandoned buildings and perusing secondhand shops.

Vonnie Winslow Crist is an award-winning author/illustrator. Her fantastical stories, poems, and art are published in Australia, Japan, India, Italy, Spain, Germany, Finland, Canada, the UK and USA. For more info: http://www.vonniewinslowcrist.com

Grace Joy Howarth is a playwright, author and composer from London. Her work has been produced in scratch nights across the UK, and she self-produced a radio play 'Until We Can't See the Sky' on Resonance FM and Chapel FM. She has had over a dozen short stories published, holds a First Class degree in Songwriting, and works as a freelance sustainability writer.

Pamela Love was born in New Jersey, and worked as a teacher and in marketing before becoming a writer. Her work has appeared in various children's publications. She is a member of the SCBWI, and won that organization's 2020 Magazine Merit Fiction Award for "The Fog Test", which appeared in Cricket. She lives in Maryland.

Terena Elizabeth Bell is a fiction writer. Her debut short story collection for adults, *Tell Me What You See,* published in December 2022. She lives in New York City, but grew up in Sinking Fork, Kentucky near Land

Between the Lakes, where "Goodbye, Nathan, Goodbye" takes place.

Grant Swenson is an aerospace engineer, working in the satellite industry, who loves writing fantasy and science-fiction for all ages. Over the last decade, his plays have been featured by various theater groups in Colorado. He is an active member of SCBWI.

Brad Jensen is an American expat living and working in Bavaria who usually writes near-future science fiction short stories. However, he is also relentlessly compelled nightly to produce middle-grade fiction for his daughter, Lyla, and it is about time he got around to writing them down. Brad recently received a Reader's Choice Award from Amazing Stories Magazine.

Michael Barbato-Dunn is an author who worked for many years as a reporter at an all-new radio station. He now toils at a public relations agency. His passions include fantasy baseball and science fiction, and he has managed to combine both in his steampunk novel, "Lord Bart and the Leagues of SIP and ALE," published in 2016 by Setheridge Press. He lives with his wife, daughter and their three dogs in Philadelphia. Find him at michaelbarbatodunn.com.

Diane Callahan strives to capture her sliver of the universe through writing fiction, nonfiction, and poetry. As a fiction editor, she spends her days shaping stories. Her YouTube channel, *Quotidian Writer,* provides practical tips for aspiring authors. You can read her work in *Consequence, The Fieldstone Review, Translunar Travelers Lounge, Tales to Terrify, Short Édition,* and *The Sunlight Press,* among others. You'll also find her musings about speculative fiction on Tor.com.

Corey Elizabeth Jackson has had her poetry published in numerous issues of Verse Afire by The Ontario Poetry Society, as well as in Blue Unicorn Journal of Poetry (California), The Society of Classical Poets (New York) and WestWard Quarterly (Illinois). She lives in Aurora, Ontario and is currently writing an illustrated book of poetry entitled Extraterrestrials Congregate

Lisa Timpf's speculative poetry has appeared in a variety of magazines and anthologies, including New Myths, Star*Line, Eye to the Telescope, Liquid Imagination, and Polar Borealis. When not writing, Lisa enjoys organic gardening, bird-watching, and walking her lively Jack Russel-cocker spaniel Chet. You can find out more about Lisa's writing at http://lisatimpf.blogspot.com/.

Guy Belleranti writes fiction, non-fiction, poetry, puzzles and humor for both children and adults. His children's writing has appeared in many publications including Highlights for Children, Short Edition, Fun For Kidz, Jack and Jill, Humpty Dumpty, and Spaceports & Spidersilk. In addition, he's had fiction, nonfiction, poetry and puzzles published by educational publishers such as ProQuest, Super Teacher Worksheets, Schoolwide and MATH Worksheets 4 Kids. Guy also has had six leveled reader books published by RR Books (aka Reading Reading Books). He worked for many years in school libraries. He is also a long-time docent educator at the local zoo. His author's website is http://guy-belleranti.weebly.com/

Douglas M. Jones, MFA University of Idaho, Literature Department Chair at The Cambridge School, San Diego, has published poetry in Antiphon, Valparaiso Poetry Review, Lullwater Review, River Oak Review, and The California Quarterly.

Lauren McBride finds inspiration in faith, family, nature, science and membership in the Science Fiction & Fantasy Poetry Association (SFPA). Nominated for the Best of the Net, Rhysling and Dwarf Stars Awards, her work has appeared in dozens of publications including Asimov's, Fantasy & Science Fiction, and Star*Line. She enjoys swimming, gardening, baking, reading, writing and knitting scarves for our troops.

www.ingramcontent.com/pod-product-compliance
Lightning Source LLC
LaVergne TN
LVHW010409070526
838199LV00065B/5923